*For everyone
who loves cats,
especially
Marni*

First published 1992 by Walker Books Ltd
87 Vauxhall Walk, London SE11 5HJ

© 1992 Sarah Hayes

First printed 1992
Printed and bound in Hong Kong by
South China Printing Co. (1988) Ltd

British Library Cataloguing in Publication Data
A catalogue record for this book
is available from the British Library
ISBN 0-7445-2173-4

THE CATS OF TIFFANY STREET

Written and illustrated by

Sarah Hayes

WALKER BOOKS

LONDON

On Friday night they arranged to meet
down at the end of Tiffany Street.
They climbed out of windows,
squeezed through doors, and one
came down from the seventh floor.
There was Marmalade Ned
with his special fish head,
Captain Bligh who had only one eye.
Delicate Fan from Isfahan,
Pitter and Pat the family cats,
and Shadow the stray
who wandered all day
searching and searching
for somewhere to stay.

Round and round to a silent beat
   they danced at the end of Tiffany Street.

Then along came the man with the van.

He snatched up Ned
and Delicate Fan

and pushed them into
the back of the van.

He snatched up Pitter.
He snatched up Pat

and Captain Bligh
the one-eyed cat.

Shadow the stray who wandered all day
quietly quietly slipped away
and hid from the man with the van.

But when the van left Tiffany Street
Shadow was hiding under the seat.

KK 104843

The man in the van drove all night
    on and on until it got light
        when he reached an empty turkey shed...

and there he shut poor Marmalade Ned
and Delicate Fan and Pitter and Pat
and Captain Bligh the one-eyed cat.

Shadow the stray who wandered all day
quietly quietly slipped away
and hid from the man with the van.

But when he lay down on his put-you-up bed
Shadow sang out from the roof of the shed,
"Never again will the cats all meet
to dance at the end of Tiffany Street."

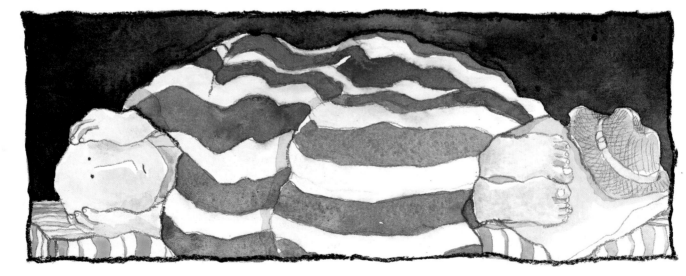

And all night long she sang that song.
And all night long he heard that song
and tossed and turned in his put-you-up bed
and thought of the cats in the turkey shed.
And when he couldn't take any more...

the man threw open the turkey-shed door.
Delicate Fan just ran and ran
but Captain Bligh attacked the man.

Pitter and Pat hissed and spat
and Marmalade Ned sat on his head.

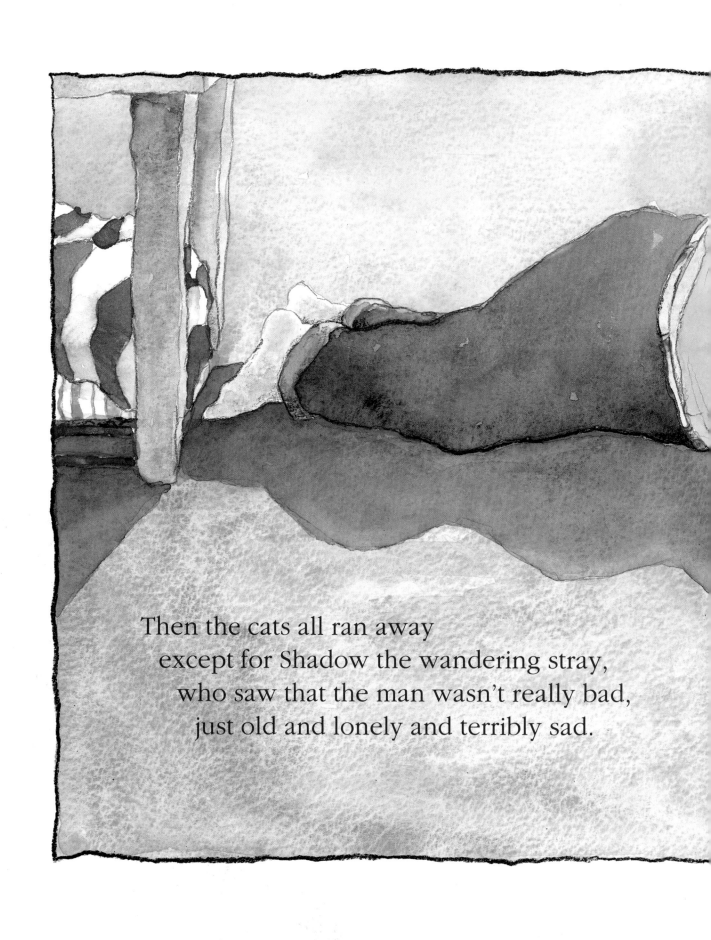

Then the cats all ran away
except for Shadow the wandering stray,
who saw that the man wasn't really bad,
just old and lonely and terribly sad.

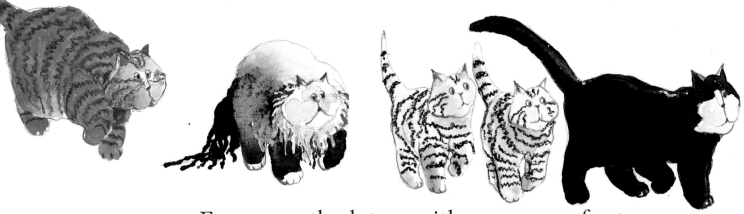

Four months later, with very sore feet,
the cats returned to Tiffany Street.

Marmalade Ned got a new fish head.
Delicate Fan ate chicken and ham.
Pitter and Pat did this and that
and Captain Bligh had pickerel pie.

And when they met on Tiffany Street
and danced and danced to the silent beat,
the cats all thought of that awful day
and wondered what happened to Shadow the stray.

Shadow was far from Tiffany Street
in a place she had found with plenty to eat
and a home and a lap and a put-you-up bed
with the man in the van and the turkey shed.